THE SECRET LIFE OF
WALTER KITTY

Story and pictures by JOAN ELIZABETH GOODMAN

A GOLDEN BOOK • NEW YORK
Western Publishing Company, Inc., Racine, Wisconsin 53404

W9-BHP-688

"Hey, Walter! Walter Kitty!" yelled Tanner Rabbit. "You left your gym suit in the drinking fountain. Walter!"

But Walter Kitty didn't hear a word as he drifted home from school. He was lost in his favorite daydream:

The amazing Walter Wonder Cat leaps into the air and rescues the baby from a perilous perch. All the citizens of Belleville shout, "Hooray! Hooray for Walter Wonder Cat! The Hero of Belleville! The Pride of . . ."

"Look out, Walter!" said Freddy the newsboy, but not soon enough. Walter and Freddy landed in a tangle on the sidewalk.

"Sorry, Freddy," said Walter. "What's the news?"

"Walter Kitty, where have you been?" asked Freddy. He handed Walter a copy of the *Daily Bulletin*.

The headline said:

No News is Good News!
Vol. XXXV No. 29
15¢

Daily Bulletin

TROUBLE IN BELLEVILLE

Badgers Run Wild!

Mayor Declares Park Unsafe!

NICK

ARTHUR
Mayor is Mad!
trash, trash &
trash.

MURRAY

ROGER
Stinky, loud, loud, and
noisy. All night long!
Police Dog can't
cope!
"It's a mess."
Only hope in

"Now this looks like a job for Wonder Cat," thought Walter.

"Thanks for the news, Freddy," said Walter as he dashed off to change into his Wonder Cat clothes.

"Ooops," said Walter. "Sorry, Mrs. Gattini."

"Walter Kitty, you are a clumsy menace!" said Mrs. Gattini. "Come back here and pick up my kumquats."

"Kumquats!" thought Walter. "I have more important work to do."

Walter raced through the back door into the kitchen, where Mama Kitty was making soup.

"Walter," said Mama, "please run down to Jake's Market and get a pound of fish heads. Then come right back and do your homework. And Walter, stay clear of the park and those horrid badgers!"

"Oh, bat knuckles," said Walter when he got to his room. "Heroes don't have time for errands." Walter put on his cape and adjusted his mask. Now he was the great, the amazing . . .

WALTER WONDER CAT!

He tiptoed past Mama and headed straight for the park.

Pete the police dog and Mayor Barclay were standing guard at the entrance. Walter ducked behind some bushes to listen to what they were saying.

"No one can sleep at night with those fiendish badgers carrying on and digging tunnels all over Belleville," said Mayor Barclay. "And look at the mess they've made of our park. You've got to get rid of them."

"I've tried, sir," said Pete. "But they just laugh at me and throw more garbage."

"Sounds like a tough job," thought Walter. "But no job is too tough for Wonder Cat!"

Walter crept along the ground until he found a good spot to crawl under the fence. He wriggled and squirmed until he came out in the park playground, right behind the castle.

"Aha!" thought Walter. "A perfect lookout post."
Walter huffed and puffed up the rope ladder.
"This is worse than gym class," he thought. At last he made
it to the top.

Walter peered over the castle wall and looked down. There was the whole nasty gang of badgers in a grisly, snoring heap. Suddenly Walter forgot all about being Wonder Cat. He just felt like wimpy Walter Kitty. "They really do look mean," thought Walter. "I wish I were home."

Walter backed away from the wall and tripped on his cape.
He stumbled into the castle slide.

"Agh!" screamed Walter. And down he went.

Kerplop! He landed right on top of Roger Badger. Roger woke up howling. As he struggled to his feet, he pulled Arthur Badger's tail. Arthur whirled around and bopped Murray Badger's snout. Murray pushed Nick Badger into the sandbox. Within seconds there was a full-scale riot.

Walter slipped through the snarling badgers and huddled under the seesaw.

The fighting got worse. The badgers roared and bellowed. The air was thick with fur. "Being a hero isn't what it's cracked up to be," thought Walter. "I'd rather be doing my homework." But Walter was too scared to move.

Finally the noise stopped. Walter peeked out from his shelter. The once-fierce badgers were now bruised and whimpering.

"Hopping Hippopotami!" said Mayor Barclay, arriving on the scene with Pete. "Look at what you've done."

"Who, me?" said Walter. "I was just leaving."

Walter darted past Mayor Barclay and raced home. When he got to his room, he ripped off his mask and cape and threw them into the closet.

"Phew," he said. "What a relief to take off that hero suit and be plain old Walter Kitty."

"Walter," said Mama Kitty, coming into his room, "where are my fish heads?"

"Oh, rat knees!" said Walter. "I guess that *is* a job for Walter Kitty."

Back at the park, Mayor Barclay looked at the fallen badgers.

"I don't know how he did it," said the mayor, "but that little cat has saved our town. What was his name?"

"I don't know," said Pete. "But from now on he will be known as the Hero of Belleville."